MOving Again!!!
With Rylan and Henry

Written and Illustrated by
Christy Jordan Wrenn

AuthorHouse™
1663 Liberty Drive
Bloomington, IN 47403
www.authorhouse.com
Phone: 1 (800) 839-8640

Published by AuthorHouse 11/19/2019
Book #3 of The Rylan Series

ISBN: 978-1-5462-4657-2 (sc)
ISBN: 978-1-5462-4658-9 (e)

This is a work of fiction, Names, Characters, businesses, places, events, locales, and incidents are either the products of the author's imagination or used in a fictitious manner. Any resemblance to actual persons, living or dead, or actual events is purely coincidental.

https://www.thebookdesigner.com/2010/01/6-copyright-page-disclaimers-and-giving-credit/

Library of Congress Control Number: 2018906976

Print information available on the last page.

Any people depicted in stock imagery provided by Getty Images are models, and such images are being used for illustrative purposes only.
Certain stock imagery © Getty Images.

This book is printed on acid-free paper.

Because of the dynamic nature of the Internet, any web addresses or links contained in this book may have changed since publication and may no longer be valid. The views expressed in this work are solely those of the author and do not necessarily reflect the views of the publisher, and the publisher hereby disclaims any responsibility for them.

authorHOUSE®

This book is dedicated to

military families everywhere who move

thousands of miles each year.

Chapter one

Rylan played outside with his scooter. Henry, his friend the mouse was always around somewhere. Rylan looked for Henry. "There he is!" Rylan smiled. He was so glad he found Henry under his bed eating chips. Henry was fun to play with and talk to, but Rylan had been thinking about Dad all day. Dad was out of the country working!

Rylan rode up

and down the driveway

thinking about his Dad.

3

Mom opened the door to say, "No riding in the street!"

Rylan waved to Mom and continued to think about
all the great things he and Dad did together.

He and dad went fishing,

mowed the lawn,

worked on the four-wheeler,

and played basketball.

Dad had even been teaching him to ride his bike.

"Rylan! Time to come eat."

"Yes ma'am," Rylan called back. He put up his scooter and helmet in the garage as Henry scampered off somewhere.

Rylan ran into the kitchen to see both of his sisters eating dinner. "Yum!" Rylan mumbled as he hung his jacket on the kitchen coat hook. "Meatloaf and mashed potatoes. I need a fork!" exclaimed Rylan.

Just as everyone began to talk about their school day, the front door slowly opened and slammed shut. Bam! Everyone looked at each other with wide eyes. They were not expecting anyone.

Who could it be?

"DAD?" everyone questioned at the same time. Olivia almost fell out of her chair rushing into the living room to be first to get to Dad. She threw her zebra one way and tiny hand-toys another. She grabbed Dad by his leg to give him a huge hug.

Mom smiled and hugged Dad. Rylan said, "Dad, you are finally home!" Dad put his cap on Rylan's head and gave him a hug. It was Emma's turn to smile and gave Dad a big kiss on the cheek.

"Yay!" Rylan thought. "Dad is back from deployment." The family is very happy to have him home.

Dad said, "Rylan come help me carry my suitcase and backpack into the guest room. You can help me unpack tomorrow. I need a shower and clean clothes." Rylan hugged Dad again before they went down the hall. Rylan saw Henry digging into an unzipped pocket in Dad's bag, probably looking for chips.

Chapter two

Dad and Mom were sitting at the kitchen table talking. They stopped talking as the kids came in the door.

"Who's in trouble?" wondered Rylan.

Dad happily said, "Mom and I have something to tell you."

"We will be moving to a new home," said Mom.

Rylan thought, "This will be the family's third move. Did every family move as much as we did?"

Emma, the oldest asked, "Where, where?"

Little Olivia chimed in, "Where?"

Rylan was quiet.

It was Mom's turn to talk, "We'll be moving back to the 'Lower 48 States' to South Carolina."

All the kids shouted at once, "Where is that?"

Emma asked, "Is that near Louisiana? I want to see our family more. Alaska is too far away!"

Mom explained, "Yes, we will be much closer to everyone. We can go visit on holidays."

Dad looked at Mom and said, "See, that wasn't too hard."

"They seemed OK with the news," Mom said to Dad.

"South Carolina, here we come," Dad announced.

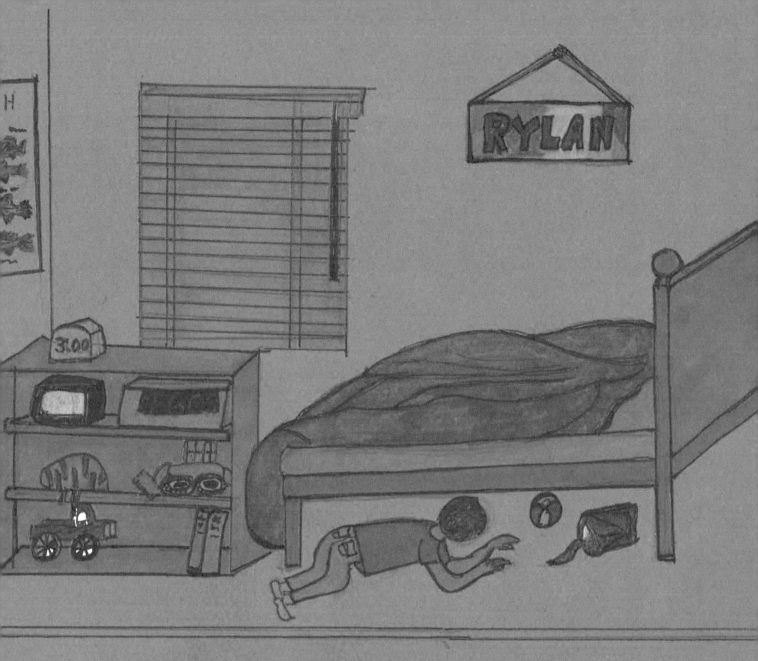

Chapter three

Rylan sat in his room thinking about moving away. He suddenly wondered, "What will happen to Henry? Will Henry want to leave Alaska to move with the family? Where is Henry?"

"Crunch, crunch, crunch."

There he was; his tail was sticking out of a chip bag.

"Henry!" Rylan exclaimed.

"Squeak!" chirped Henry. The mouse poked his nose out and back in as Emma rushed into Rylan's room.

Emma was excited, "Rylan, you have to bring all of your building projects, trucks, cars, clothes, toys, and everything!"

Rylan looked at her with wide eyes, as his stomach made a flip-flop. "I don't think, I want to move," Rylan said to himself.

Emma threw up her hands as she rushed out of Rylan's room, "You better pick up that chip bag before Mom sees it."

Rylan reached down to see if Henry was still in the chip bag. Henry crawled out to greet Rylan with another, "Squeak!"

"Hi Henry," Rylan greeted the mouse.

There in his room, Rylan explained to Henry that the family was moving to a place called South Carolina where everything would be new and exciting.

Henry replied, "Squeak?" and went back under the bed to find another chip.

"Now, how are we going to get you there?" Rylan said to the hungry mouse.

"Henry, you will just have to ride in my backpack," Rylan said as he began to pile up things to pack.

Chapter four

Mom and Dad were all excited about moving. A lot of things had to be done. Everyone would travel in Mom's truck from Alaska, through Canada to South Carolina.

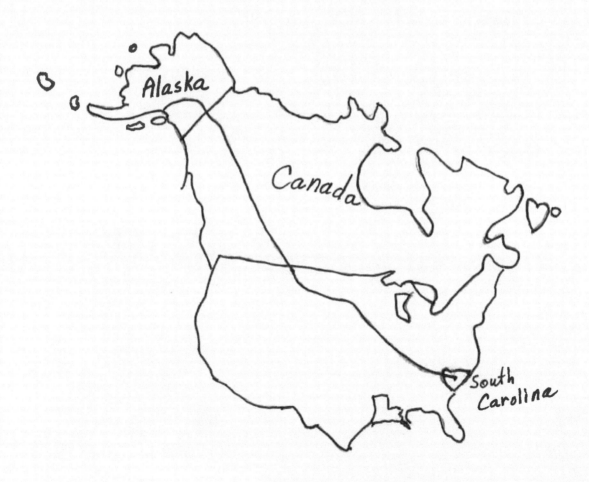

"What would happen to all their furniture, toys, cloths, kitchen things, Dad's boat and four-wheeler? How would all that get to South Carolina in Mom's truck?" thought Rylan.

One morning Rylan heard Mom talking on her cell phone about a moving truck to come pick up their things. "Wow!" Rylan said out loud. "Is that how families move?" Rylan exclaimed. "I need to get my things ready. I do not want to leave anything behind."

"Mom, what can I put my stuff in to move," asked Rylan?

Mom said, "Don't worry about that Ry. The movers pack up everything in boxes. You, Emma, and Olivia will have your favorite toys, e-readers, games, books, DVDs, and favorite treats in your backpacks."

"Perfect for Henry," Rylan thought and then smiled.

"Mom, we will need lots of chips," reminded Rylan.

Rylan asked, "Will we be spending the night in a hotel?"

Mom said, "Oh, yes! We will drive 4,421 miles and spend eight days and nights on the road to get to our new home."

Rylan was not sure what all that meant, so he just said, "OK!"

Chapter five

Rylan had not seen Henry in several days. "The moving truck is coming today. Where is Henry? What will Henry do if he is left behind or packed in a box?" Everyone was busy getting ready to leave for South Carolina. The moving truck was packed and gone.

Mom had put backpacks filled with each child's favorite things and plenty of snacks in the truck. The ice chest was filled with drinks. All the suitcases were stored under the truck seats and the four-wheeler was in the back.

Suddenly, Mom and Dad both said, "OK, let's go! We have a long drive to our new house." Rylan was buckled in his seat. Dad buckled Olivia in her seat. Emma was arguing about something with Mom as she buckled up. Off they want, saying good-bye to four years spent in Anchorage, Alaska.

Dad said something to Mom about driving 553 miles each day. Rylan thought, "that number is big." He was not sure since he was only five.

The family had not traveled far before Emma read a sign, "Welcome to Canada."

Rylan wondered, "What is Canada?"

Days passed into nights as Rylan and his family traveled the Alaskan Highway to the "Lower 48 states." One day the family stopped to eat an early lunch in Whitehorse. Rylan just knew there would be white horses to pet there. He looked and looked but no white horses.

Stopping at a restaurant in the mountains, the family went inside to eat. Everyone ordered their favorite meal. Emma wanted chicken strips and fries. Olivia wanted macaroni and cheese. Rylan ordered chicken nuggets and fries, but he was not hungry. He wanted to be home, back in Alaska, in his upstairs room building something or watching a DVD. Everyone was eating, except Rylan.

Dad said, "Eat!"

Mom said, "Eat!"

Bossy Emma said, "Eat!"

Rylan started to cry. He wanted to go back home to Alaska.

Mom hugged Rylan and said, "Don't cry. We will find a nice hotel where we can rest. Rylan, you need to eat, or you will be hungry before bedtime." He ate a little.

Chapter six

The next morning Rylan was so hungry. He ordered chocolate chip pancakes with whipped cream, eggs and lots of bacon. "Yum!"

The family soon got back into the truck again. Driving down a long mountain road, Rylan looked up and said, "Dad, what are those?"

Dad said, "Buffalo!"

The family took a short lunch and was back in the truck and on their way. Miles and miles of highway passed under the truck tires. Rylan looked out the window to see a lake. "Dad, can we stop and fish?"

Dad smiled and said, "Not now, but when we get to South Carolina, you and I will go fishing. I promise!"

The truck rounded a bend in the road. Rylan and the girls said, "Wow!" at the same time. Just in front of the truck was a herd of big horned sheep.

Mom, exclaimed, "Look! there is a big moose down the road."

Rylan was not impressed. He had seen moose, bears, and wolves near their house in Alaska.

Emma exclaimed, "That sign says, Welcome to the United States of America!"

"Mom, are we almost to our new home?" asked Olivia. She had been quiet the whole trip. "No, we are still a long way from our new home. We have about 2,200 miles to go."

Chapter seven

Rylan had forgotten all about Henry. Rylan did not know that Henry had hitched a ride on the four-wheeler in the back of Mom's truck. Henry was having a great time finding food at restaurants and hotels where the family stopped. He always jumped back into the truck, just in time.

Grape
Soda

Rylan overheard Mom and Dad talking as he fell asleep. They said that the trip would be over soon. Eight days on the road was too long for three children, Mom and Dad, and of course, a mouse named Henry.

The next morning as the family loaded back into the truck, Dad said, "Kids, this is our last day of traveling. We will be in South Carolina tonight."

The kids seemed too tired to say anything. They just kept busy.

Rylan was ready to get out of the truck and see what his new room looked like. He wondered, "Would all of my toys be there?"

"Mom, what does our new house look like?"

Mom and Dad were both quiet. She finally said, "We don't know yet. The real-estate lady will have some houses for us to see tomorrow. We will pick one to live in then."

Rylan and Emma looked at Mom and Dad with wide eyes. They both whispered, "We do not have a place to live, yet? Oh, no!"

Dad told the family that they would be staying in the hotel on the base where dad was going to work. Rylan felt better already. He would see his new home and room tomorrow.

Chapter eight

Early in the morning, Mom got a call from the house lady. Back into the truck they went to find a new house.

Soon Dad drove into the driveway of a nice, red brick house. The house was big. The backyard was big. Rylan could see himself running and playing with his sisters in the backyard. The whole family loved their new home.

Rylan had a sad thought, "Where is my stuff?"

Mom said, "The moving truck will be here tomorrow."

Rylan liked it, "a new house with my toys on the way."

The next day, Dad asked Rylan to get something from the truck. As Rylan opened the truck door, guess who appeared? Rylan said, "HENRY! How did you get here?"

Henry just gave a happy, "Squeak!"

Everything was complete for Rylan's family. He was so happy about the new house. They had moved 4,421 miles and are still all together, even Henry!

Rylan snickered to himself, "Henry and I will have some great fun in our big backyard. I cannot wait to swing on the horse, tree swing hanging in the big tree."

THE END.

Christy Jordan Wrenn is a professional librarian, children's picture book author and grandparent. Forty plus years of librarianship has prepared her greatly for writing and illustrating for children. Over the past seven years, Christy has become a self-taught illustrator and writer of picture books. She has published three picture books: Rylan and Burt (2014), Rylan and Henry (2015), and Emma's Funny Birds (2016). The first two Rylan books and this new book Moving Again!!! With Rylan and Henry are all a part of her Rylan Series of books. Her grandchildren Rylan, Emma, and Olivia were their Gran's inspiration to share their Alaskan adventures and creative minds with other children.

https://www.amazon.com/Christy-Jordan-Wrenn/e/
B00OR2DPPO/ref=sr_ntt_srch_lnk_1?qid=1529090880&sr=1-1

Thanks for reading! If you enjoyed this book or found it useful I'd be very grateful if you'd post a short review on Amazon about how useful you found my book. Your support really does make a difference and I read all the reviews personally so I can get your feedback and make my books even better.

Printed in the United States
By Bookmasters